The HARE and the HEDGEHOG

Axel Scheffler

Retold by Axel Scheffler and Alison Green

It was a beautiful summer's day, and the whole world was in a good mood. Hedgehog sat in his neat little garden, whistling a tune. Not everyone liked his whistling, but Hedgehog didn't mind. He'd got his children all washed and dressed, and was ready to trot down to the field to check on his turnips.

They weren't actually *his* turnips, but as no one knew who the field belonged to, Hedgehog nipped in now and then and helped himself.

He hadn't gone far when he bumped into Hare. "Morning!" said Hedgehog politely.

Hare looked him up and down snootily. "Where are you off to?" he sneered.

"I'm going for a walk," said Hedgehog.

"A walk! With those little legs?" laughed Hare.

Hedgehog was rather upset. He did have little legs, but he was very happy with them. "I suppose you think your legs are better than mine?" he said.

"I should think so!" snorted Hare.

Hedgehog was so cross he blurted out, "Then why don't we run a race? I bet you my little legs will beat your great long ones!"

"Sure," laughed Hare. "Let's start right now. I can't wait to tell the whole world about the silly little hedgehog who thought he could beat a hare!"

Oh no! What had Hedgehog done? He'd landed himself in a pickle, and no mistake.

"Hang on!" he squeaked. "I haven't had breakfast yet. I'll see you back here in half an hour."

Then he ran home as fast as his little hedgehog legs could carry him.

Hedgehog burst through his garden gate, totally out of puff.

"Oh, my dear wife!" he cried. "What am I to do? I told Hare I could beat him in a race. With his great long legs! I'll be a laughing stock all over town when he tells everyone: the silly little hedgehog who thought he could outrun a hare!"

This was a pickle indeed. Mrs Hedgehog racked her brains. They needed a good plan, and fast!

Then, "I've got it!" she cried. She ran to the dresser and pulled on one of Hedgehog's white shirts and a pair of his blue dungarees. Hedgehog gasped. Suddenly his wife looked just like him!

"Come on!" said Mrs Hedgehog. "Quick!" And she dragged her puzzled husband out of the house.

As they trotted to the turnip field, Mrs Hedgehog ran through her plan.

"Listen carefully!" she said. "Tell Hare you're going to run the race in the big, long field. He'll run in one furrow, and you'll run in another. Start at the top of the field, and I'll hide at the bottom of the field. When Hare gets close, I'll jump up and shout, 'Beat you!' Hare will think that I'm you, and that you've run the whole way. Got it?"

Hedgehog scratched his head. "Got it," he said, though he wasn't sure he had.

When they arrived at the field, Mrs Hedgehog hid behind a bush down at the bottom.

Hedgehog trotted to the top of the field, where he found Hare waiting for him. He was dressed in his trendy running gear and was hopping about impatiently.

"Ready?" said Hare, gazing up at the clouds as if Hedgehog wasn't even there.

"Ready!" said Hedgehog, trying to sound more confident than he felt.

They lined up at the start, and Hare made a great show of waggling his little tail about like a proper runner.

Then Hedgehog squeaked, "One, twooooo, THREE – GO!" and Hare shot off down the field like a cannonball.

Hedgehog trotted behind for a few steps – then dropped to the ground and crouched down in his furrow.

When Hare arrived at the bottom of the field, Mrs Hedgehog popped up and shouted, "Beat you!"

Hare was amazed. "Race you back to the start!" he snapped, and he bounded back at top speed.

Hare ran so fast his floppity ears streamed out behind him. But just before he reached the top of the field, up popped Hedgehog calling, "Beat you again!"

Hare gasped in astonishment. "Race you back down again!" he panted.

"Sure," smiled Hedgehog. "As many times as you wish!"

Hare ran up and down that field seventy-four times. But every single time he approached the finishing line, up popped a calm little hedgehog crying, "Beat you!"

Poor, silly Hare! On the seventy-fifth time, he staggered down the field – and flopped to the ground at Mrs Hedgehog's feet. He couldn't go another step.

Mrs Hedgehog felt a bit sorry for snooty old Hare, even if he had been mean to her husband.

She called for help, and Hare soon started to feel better. But he never did work out Mrs Hedgehog's clever trick. And he was never snooty to a hedgehog ever again.

As for Mr and Mrs Hedgehog, they scampered home in high spirits. Then they packed a picnic, fetched their children and sat on a sunny green hill to enjoy the rest of the day.

Published in the UK by Alison Green Books, 2023
An imprint of Scholastic

1 London Bridge, London SE1 9BG
Scholastic Ireland, 89E Lagan Road, Dublin Industrial
Estate, Glasnevin, Dublin, D11 HP5F

First published in German under the title: *Hase und Igel*
Published by arrangement with Julius Beltz GmbH & Co. KG.

ISBN: 9780702318290

A CIP catalogue record for this book is
available from the British Library.

Printed in China

Paper made from wood grown in sustainable
forests and other controlled sources.

10 9 8 7 6 5 4 3 2 1

www.scholastic.co.uk

MIX
Paper | Supporting
responsible forestry
FSC® C008047